The Fire Station

The Fire Station

STORY by
ROBERT MUNSCH

ART by
MICHAEL MARTCHENKO

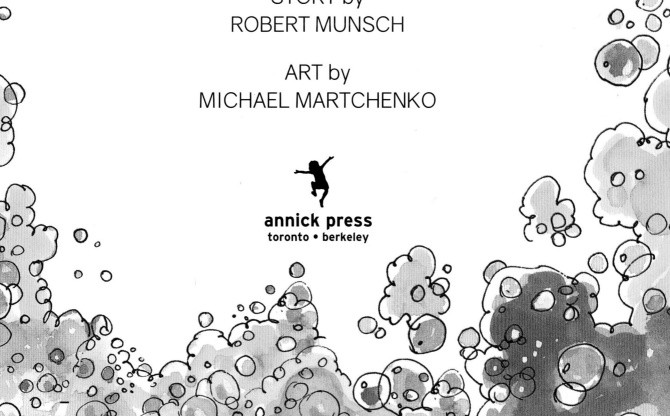

annick press
toronto • berkeley

We acknowledge the support of the Canada Council for the Arts and the Ontario Arts Council, and the participation of the Government of Canada/la participation du gouvernement du Canada for our publishing activities.

Library and Archives Canada Cataloguing in Publication

Munsch, Robert N., 1945-, author
     The fire station / Robert Munsch ; [illustrations by] Michael Martchenko.

(Classic Munsch)
Previously published: Toronto : Annick Press, ©1983.
ISBN 978-1-77321-081-0 (hardcover).--ISBN 978-1-77321-080-3 (softcover)

     I. Martchenko, Michael, illustrator II. Title.

PS8576.U575F5 2018   jC813'.54   C2018-901420-2

Published in the U.S.A. by Annick Press (U.S.) Ltd.
Distributed in Canada by University of Toronto Press.
Distributed in the U.S.A. by Publishers Group West.

Printed in China

www.annickpress.com
www.robertmunsch.com

Also available in e-book format. Please visit www.annickpress.com/ebooks.html for more details.

To Holly Martchenko, Toronto, Ontario
and to Michael Villamore and
Sheila Prescott, Coos Bay, Oregon

Michael and Sheila were walking down the street. As they passed the fire station Sheila said, "Michael! Let's go ride a fire truck."

"Well," said Michael, "I think maybe I should ask my mother, and I think maybe I should ask my father, and I think maybe . . ."

"I think we should go in," said Sheila. Then she grabbed Michael's hand and pulled him up to the door.

Sheila knocked:
BLAM-BLAM-BLAM-BLAM-BLAM.

A large firefighter came out and asked, "What can I do for you?"

"Well," said Michael, "maybe you could show us a fire truck and hoses and rubber boots and ladders and all sorts of stuff like that."

"Certainly," said the firefighter.

"And maybe," said Sheila, "you will let us drive a fire truck?"

"Certainly not," said the firefighter.

They went in and looked at ladders and hoses and big rubber boots. Then they looked at little fire trucks and big fire trucks and enormous fire trucks. When they were done Michael said, "Let's go."

"Right," said Sheila. "Let's go into the enormous fire truck."

While they were in the truck, the fire alarm went off:
CLANG-CLANG-CLANG-CLANG-CLANG.

"Oh, no!" said Michael.

"Oh, yes!" said Sheila. Then she grabbed Michael and pulled him into the back seat.

Firefighters came running from all over. They slid down poles and ran down stairs. Then they jumped onto the truck and drove off. The firefighters didn't look in the back seat. Michael and Sheila were in the back seat.

They came to an enormous fire. Lots of yucky-colored smoke got all over everything. It colored Michael yellow, green, and blue. It colored Sheila purple, green, and yellow.

When the fire chief saw them he said, "What are you doing here!"

Sheila said, "We came in the fire truck. We thought maybe it was a bus. We thought maybe it was a taxi. We thought maybe it was an elevator. We thought maybe . . ."

"I think maybe I'd better take you home," said the fire chief. He put Michael and Sheila in his car and drove them away.

When Michael got home he knocked on the door. His mother opened it and said, "You messy boy! You can't come in and play with Michael! You're too dirty." She slammed the door right in Michael's face.

"My own mother," said Michael. "She didn't even know me."
He knocked on the door again.

His mother opened the door and said, "You dirty boy! You
can't come in and play with Michael. You're too dirty. You're
absolutely filthy. You're a total mess. You're . . . Oh, my!
. . . Oh, no! . . . YOU'RE MICHAEL!"

Michael went inside and lived in the bathtub for three days until
he got clean.

When Sheila came home she knocked on the door. Her father opened it and saw an incredibly messy girl. He said, "You can't come in to play with Sheila. You're too dirty." He slammed the door right in her face.

"Ow," said Sheila. "My own father and he didn't even know me."

She kicked and pounded on the door as loudly as she could. Her father opened the door and said, "Now stop that racket, you dirty girl. You can't come in to play with Sheila. You're too dirty. You're absolutely filthy. You're a total mess. You're . . . Oh, my! . . . Oh, no! . . . YOU'RE SHEILA!"

"Right," said Sheila, "I went to a fire in the back of a fire truck and I got all smoky. I WASN'T EVEN SCARED."

Sheila went inside and lived in the bathtub for five days until she got clean.

Then Michael took Sheila on a walk past the police station. He told her, "If you ever take me in another fire truck, I am going to ask the police to put you in jail."

"**JAIL!**" yelled Sheila. "Let's go look at the jail! What a great idea!"

"Oh, no!" yelled Michael, and Sheila grabbed his hand and pulled him into the police station.

Even More Classic Munsch:

Classic Munsch ABC
The Dark
Mud Puddle
The Paper Bag Princess
The Boy in the Drawer
Jonathan Cleaned Up—Then He Heard a Sound
Millicent and the Wind
Mortimer
Murmel, Murmel, Murmel
Angela's Airplane
David's Father
Thomas' Snowsuit
50 Below Zero
I Have to Go!
Moira's Birthday
A Promise is a Promise
Pigs
Something Good
Show and Tell
Purple, Green and Yellow
Wait and See
Where is Gah-Ning?
From Far Away
Stephanie's Ponytail
Munschworks: The First Munsch Collection
Munschworks 2: The Second Munsch Treasury
Munschworks 3: The Third Munsch Treasury
Munschworks 4: The Fourth Munsch Treasury
The Munschworks Grand Treasury
Munsch Mini-Treasury One
Munsch Mini-Treasury Two
Munsch Mini-Treasury Three

For information on these titles please visit www.annickpress.com
Many Munsch titles are available in French and/or Spanish, as well as in
board book and e-book editions. Please contact your favorite supplier.